My Special Brother Bo

britt e. collins

illustrated by **brittany bone-roth**

My Special Brother Bo

All marketing and publishing rights guaranteed to and reserved by:

FUTURE HORIZONS INC.

721 W. Abram St. Arlington, TX 76013

Toll-free: 800·489·0727 | Fax: 817·277·2270

www.FHautism.com | info@FHautism.com

Text © 2018 Britt E. Collins

Illustrations © 2018 Brittany Roth

ISBN: 9781941765920

This book is dedicated to Mary Allison, my sister who has special needs. I love you always.

– Britt

For my kind, creative, talented Annie; inquisitive, sweet, appreciative Fisher; witty, cuddly, and imaginative Britton. I love you so very much ABF!

– Brittany / Mommy

Hi! My name is Lucy and I am seven years old. I am in first grade at Mountain Elementary School. I like going to school and being in Mrs. Walker's class.

My favorite things to do at school are science and reading. I love it when we have free reading time and I can sit on the beanbags to read my favorite book.

3

I also love the science projects that we do. Last week, we made a volcano and it really erupted! It was so cool!

I live with Mommy and Daddy and my little brother, Bo. Mom says Bo is special. He goes to preschool where the teachers and therapists help him learn.

Bo doesn't really talk but I try to teach him. We play school and I'm the teacher. I write words on the chalkboard and teach him to say "Lucy." He usually just calls me "ucy" because he can't say the "L" sound.

When Bo was born he wouldn't eat, so Mommy had to feed him through a tube in his nose. Daddy always sang to us when Bo was crying or I felt scared.

When Bo was three, he went to speech therapy and
occupational therapy. They were in this big gym with balls
and swings and Bo got to play. I couldn't go in, so I had to
wait in the lobby with Mommy.

The therapists teach Bo how to eat, talk, and play with toys. He always spins the wheels on the car instead of racing them like I do.

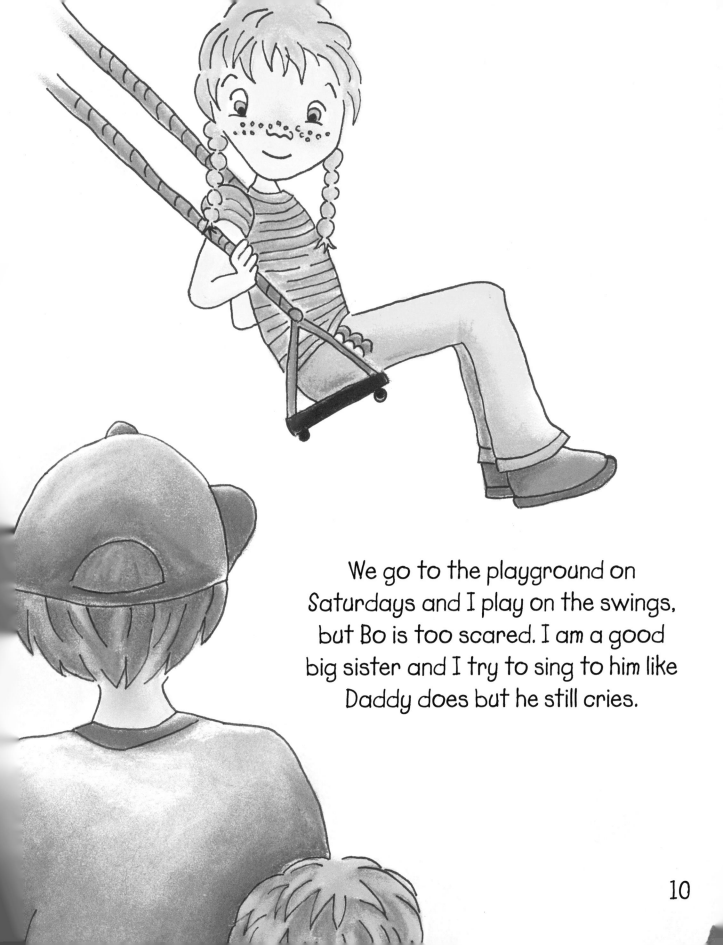

We go to the playground on Saturdays and I play on the swings, but Bo is too scared. I am a good big sister and I try to sing to him like Daddy does but he still cries.

Bo likes to play by himself. I try to get him to play chase with me, but he just runs around in circles and talks to himself in his special language.

Mommy, Daddy, and I can't understand Bo when he talks in his special language.

When I am at school I like to play with my friend Annie. She doesn't have any brothers or sisters so she always gets to do fun stuff with her mommy and daddy.

Sometimes my family can't go places because Bo cries or gets scared. One time we went to the mall and Bo began to kick and scream when we tried to take him on the carousel. I think the big horses scared him.

Since I couldn't go on the carousel by myself, we had to go home. That made me sad.

Mommy tells me that I have to be brave for Bo because he looks up to me. When summertime comes there is no more school and Bo and I get to go swimming. I teach Bo how to blow bubbles and kick his feet. He's swimming! And I helped!

Daddy says he's proud of me for teaching Bo to put his face in the water. I'm a good big sister!

14

Sometimes I don't want my friends to come over because of Bo.

He embarrasses me, but I DO love him. Mommy and Daddy say I should tell my friends Bo is special and doesn't understand things.

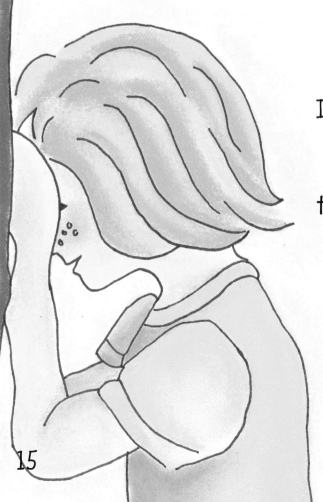

I want to make Bo happy, so I make him laugh with tickles and games.

Maybe I can let Bo play with my friends and me.

Bo gets lots of attention and I feel left out. Mommy tells me I am special too and she takes me out for ice cream.

I love my Mommy and Daddy and Bo, too. I am so glad to have a little brother who is special like Bo.

Pediatric occupational therapist Britt Collins graduated from Colorado State University over 13 years ago and since then has worked tirelessly on OT and sensory integration awareness, research, and application. Britt has worked in a variety of settings including pediatric hospital inpatient, ICU, rehabilitation, outpatient clinics, homes, schools, and skilled nursing facilities. With her award-winning OT DVD series and three books, *Sensory Parenting: Newborns to Toddlers*, *Sensory Parenting: The Elementary Years*, and her latest book, *Sensory Yoga for Kids: Therapeutic Movement for Children of all Abilities*, Britt is among the cutting-edge leaders in the field. Her books have received enthusiastic reviews from Dr. Lucy Jane Miller and Lindsey Biel M.A., OTR/L, and she presents nationwide alongside experts Temple Grandin, Paula Aquilla, Diane Bahr, and Carol Kranowitz.

Britt's professional specialties include working with children with sensory processing disorder, autism spectrum disorder, ADHD, Down syndrome, feeding disorders, and more. She is also certified to teach yoga for children with special needs ages 0–12. She is working to complete her full yoga certification and her children's yoga certification.

Currently, Britt resides outside of Memphis, TN. She has two young children that keep her busy along with writing and presenting across the country. For more information on Britt, please visit www.sensoryparenting.com and www.sensoryyogaforkids.com.

Brittany Lynn Bone-Roth loves working with kids, especially those with special needs. She has a Bachelor of Arts in Art and a Master of Arts in Curriculum and Instruction in Education with a focus on Elementary and Early Childhood Leadership. A mom of three and former first-grade teacher, Brittany enjoys creating art in a variety of mediums as well as swimming, riding bikes, and playing and reading with her kids. She has combined her creative and classroom talents with her experience as a mom to create the eye-catching illustrations that fill these pages. Brittany lives in Colorado with her family. This is her first book.

DID YOU LIKE THE BOOK?

Rate it and share your opinion.

amazon.com

BARNES&NOBLE
BOOKSELLERS
www.bn.com

Not what you expected? Tell us!

Most negative reviews occur when the book did not reach expectation. Did the description build any expectations that were not met? Let us know how we can do better.

Please drop us a line at *info@fhautism.com*.

Thank you so much for your support!

CPSIA information can be obtained
at www.ICGtesting.com
Printed in the USA
BVHW020521050119
537004BV00001B/1/P